I0609796

Charles Gildehaus, Johann Wolfgang von Goethe

In Rhyme and Time

Volume 1

Charles Gildehaus, Johann Wolfgang von Goethe

In Rhyme and Time
Volume 1

ISBN/EAN: 9783337394967

Printed in Europe, USA, Canada, Australia, Japan

Cover: Foto ©Andreas Hilbeck / pixelio.de

More available books at **www.hansebooks.com**

IN

RHYME AND TIME.

Shakespeare's Birthday.
Poems.
Translations from Goethe.

BY

CHARLES GILDEHAUS.

SAINT LOUIS:
JOHN L. BOLAND BOOK AND STATIONERY CO.,
610 WASHINGTON AV.
1895.

Concerning the original poems contained in this little volume, the author has nothing to say: these must speak for themselves or remain silent.

A word of apology or explanation, however, would seem to mitigate the arrogance attaching to any attempt at translating from Goethe. Beyond a moment's curiosity, I do not hope to please any one acquainted with the genius of the German tongue; as soon would I expect to delight an Englishman with a German translation of King Lear. To those, however, not familiar with the text of a master, who with Homer and Shakespeare completes the triumvirate of the world's greatest poets, to those I venture the assertion, that Goethe's truth is so profound, his beauty so resplendent, that even a weak translation of his lines will excel the original of many another.

Now, as to the inexorable dilemma which confronts and discourages every translator : how free, how literal shall he treat the text? Every true lover of art condemns the man who with unhallowed hand takes undue liberties with that which, by reason of its perfection, has grown sacred. And yet a literal translation, word for word, will not merely, as may be seen in some who have tried it, render many passages ridiculous, but would, if rigidly pursued, admit neither rhythm, rhyme nor metre. If to paraphrase be iniquitous, let the pedant still bear in mind, that this heinous offense undergoes no amelioration when committed against the spirit of a poem. A true translation, I doubt if there be one, proves true to both the content and the form. Whenever in my navigation through Goethe's poems I found my course endangered by this Scylla of content and this Charybdis of form, I have always, however distasteful the choice, preferred the living spirit to the dead letter.

G.

CONTENTS.

(5)

Translations from Goethe.

Some say the world's a mill wherein man's life
Like to the clattering wheels goes round and
  round
Grinding of trifles. Be that as it will,
This day we'll steal out of the busy year,
And glide on Fancy's pinion to the spot
Where Shakespeare dwelt. If we have eyes to
  see,
Strange wonders may be ours ; for on the brink
Of sedgy Avon, where old Stratford stands,
The immortal sons and daughters of the poet
Do yearly congregate, and bring to him
Their natal greetings. Most of them we'll see,
But many a noted one must need escape,
So numb'rous is the multitude of those
That celebrate to-day.

1. The Tempest.
2. A Midsummer-Night's Dream.
3. Measure for Measure.
4. The Two Gentlemen of Verona.
5. As You Like It.
6. The Winter's Tale.
7. Cymbeline.
8. The Merchant of Venice.
9. All's Well That Ends Well.
10. Much Ado About Nothing.
11. The Comedy of Errors.
12. The Taming of the Shrew.
13. Twelfth Night.
14 Love's Labour's Lost.
15. Timon of Athens.
16. Troilus and Cressida.

17. Coriolanus.
18. Julius Caesar.
19. Anthony and Cleopatra.
20. King John.
21. " Richard II.
22. " Henry IV.
23. The Merry Wives of Windsor.
24. King Henry V.
25. " Henry VI.
26. " Richard III.
27. " Henry VIII.
28. Romeo and Juliet.
29. Othello.
30. King Lear.
31. Macbeth.
32. Hamlet

(8)

SHAKESPEARE'S BIRTHDAY.

I.

Who may the leader be of this vast throng
And high festivity? It is a poet,
The image of his maker — Prospero.
With mighty arm he curbs the Caliban,
While o'er his head the host of imagery,
Exquisite Ariel and the dainty shapes
Of Fancy are a-wing. Harmoniously
Their flight is pitched in measure to his step,
And as he walks, obediently they fly.

II.

From fairy-land, from the Athenian wood,
From Summer-Night's Dream comes King
    Oberon,
And impish Puck and queen Titania
Vexéd and fretting for her stolen boy;

(9)

Theseus, the duke, with his fair Amazon,
The troubled lovers and the cruel father,
The clod-poll, Bottom, and the other asses,
Quince, Snug and Flute and Snout and
    Starveling.—
But see, what strange and supernatural things
Swarm round about us. Time is young again,
And the air breeds spirits as it did of old:
Uncanny elves with globy long-eared heads
Striding on spider legs; and fairy freaks
Of waggish mien, twisted and pressed and pulled
From all proportion; goblins and wingéd sprites
Like dragon-flies enchanted; uncouth imps
And hornéd snails, and locomotive plants,
And things that waver 'twixt the definition
Of nature's kingdoms. In bewildering flight
They fill the atmosphere; and man himself,
Entangled in their chaos of unreason,
Becomes deranged. Still, we shall find some
    method
In this profuse confusion, if we can
But shake this all-surrounding madness off
And view it from beyond, a looker-on.
Bottom, for instance, and his neighbor louts,
With asses' hoof would tread the buskin here,
While Theseus with prosaic understanding
Sits critic. Let us look at them again: —
No counterfeit for Bottom: on my life,
He knows what's what. Yes, sir; he'll have his
    moon

In body physical, or not at all;
While Theseus says, the whole affair is moon-
    shine,
And nothing more; the poet is a madman,
His art is lunacy, his whole creation
An idiot's offspring, — Theseus, that will do.
You may be wise in more than one respect,
But, mark you, as a judge of poesy
You sit not far from Bottom.

III.

Here comes Vincentio, the lenient duke,
And at his side the snowy Isabella
Who fled the lewd world and in barren cloister
Immured herself, till wisely she concluded,
That chastity, to reap her own reward,
Must interchange her virtue with another,
Be a true man's true wife.
And after them comes Angelo, the fraud,
Who posed as justice and who ravished justice,
Who sneered at mercy and who lives by mercy,
Or else had perished. Measure still for Measure
By highest court is meted out to all.

IV.

Verona's gentlemen. True Valentine
And Proteus, fickle as his name imports,

Are here at hand; two pretty damsels walk
Along by them.   And, look you, in the rear,
Lag two whom nature bred in happy mood,
Launce and his old dog, Crab.

V.

" Under the greenwood tree," list to the song,
" Who loves to lie with me," whence the gay
    throng
That sheds the perfume of delicious green
Along its path, as if young nature had
But now created them?   These are the folk
From Arden forest, who re-enter now
The world whence they were banished.   Men
    and women,
Perceive you, come in pairs.   There is the duke
With all his retinue; and there's Orlando
With arm around his charming Rosalind,
Whose merry spirits bubble o'er with laughter
And roguish joy, as she relates to him
The cunning of her pranks.   Along by them
The wise fool, Touchstone, saunters.   By that
    vague
And absent-minded look of his I know,
That in his workshop he is busy now
Whittling a bolt that will not fail to strike
Straight in the center.

VI.

Yon lady whose bewitching countenance
Seems both to invite and to repel our passion,
That is Hermione, the wife of wives:
And at her side, the monarch of Sicilia,
Once called the rash Leontes, but now purged
With fifteen years' contrition.   In their wake
Follow the flowrets of the Winter's Tale,
Sweet Perdita and constant Florizel.
Next comes the wise Camillo: he would speak,
But quick Paulina, with a tongue for two,
Says, " dear Camillo, we are partners now,
Let us divide our work, and each do that
He can do best.   I'll speak and you shall think."
A troop of gaily-spangled shepherdesses
With true Polixenes, Bohemia's king,
Completes the picture.

VII.

Here comes a ruler born in Caesar's day,
King Cymbeline of Britain.   Take no heed
Of him, nor of Pisanio, nor Posthumus,
Nor any of these mounted noblemen,
However haply you might see among them
An ancestor of yours.   Ignore them all,
Dull not the edge of your eyes' appetite
Before the feast; for in this moving billow

The pearl of the ocean dwells. O Imogen,
Soft as the breathing of thy own sweet name,
Speech can not compass thee! — Ere she was
    born
The elements of heat and cold were never
So deftly mingled. She's the miracle
Of frost and fire : Cupid's rosy torch
Nourished with untouched snow. Our common
    fires
Will heat the metal to a ruddy glow,
But, Imogen, with purer, finer passion,
Burns white, immaculate.

VIII.

The next group in our holiday procession
Is come from busy Venice. There's Antonio
The generous merchant prince, with his dear
    friend,
Bassanio, bold and dashing as a knight
Of love should be. Gratiano holds them both
With his eternal tongue ; and they must listen,
Or he will cut them with his stinging wit.
That is Lorenzo, and the pretty Jew
Is Jessica, become a Christian now.
Next comes Nerissa, and along by her
The gentle Portia walks. Observe her well ;
For we shall never meet another one
In whom the qualities of woman's virtue
Dwell in that true harmonious equipoise

As in Bassanio's wife. With tottering step
Shylock, the Jew, approaches: wiser now,
In having learned that there is more in law
Than naked justice. Justice he demanded,
And justice he received. Justice had slain him,
But mercy lets him live.

IX.

And here is Helena, whose fixéd hunger
Dared her assume the pitchy garb of shame,
And by the ugliest and unholiest means
To gain her end, her Bertram. Look, she smiles,
And to our head-shake on her doubtful method,
Says, " All is well that ends well."

X.

O Cupid, Cupid, thou art mighty yet,
For, look you, here is signior Benedict
Locked side by side in matrimony's yoke
With Beatrice, than whom there is no woman
With sharper tongue. For many a month and
      year
These poured the vials of disdainful jest
On love and family. Nor is it strange
Two scoffers so alike in hate as these
Would find some admiration for each other. —
If ever retribution came to mortal,

We have it here.   Still, they're a goodly match ;
And calumny, whose breath did almost poison
The love that Hero held from Claudio,
Might blow on Benedict and Beatrice
Until his lungs were empty. — In the press
Comes Dogberry, the justice, still proclaiming
" I am an ass; " a satire most severe
Upon the rulers and the state who failed
To find what this great blockhead stumbled on.

XI.

These are the dupes of Error's Comedy :
Two Dromios and two Antipholi,
And wives and friends and creditors and debtors
And a long train of chance acquaintances,
Who by this likeness of exterior semblance
Were cast into confusion limitless.
See, how they stare in blank bewilderment
On nature's repetition.   In good sooth,
Nor can I tell which are from Ephesus
And which from Syracusa.   Let us ask them.
Heigh, you twin clown, I pray thee, stop a
        moment
To tell us which is which, and which are you !
" Ask me no whiches, we are all bewitched;
And yet, good sir, I'll take upon myself
To show you him that hails from Syracusa,
If first you pick the clown from Ephesus."

XII.

Petruchio and his Kate, his bonny Kate;
Not wild Kate now, but meek and gentle Kate,
Whose tetchy humor and insane caprice
Lacked nothing but a glass to see it in.
Petruchio held the mirror to the shrew,
And since his medicine was like for like,
Her meekness, too, will find in him reflection,
And make him gentle.

XIII.

Twelfth Night or What you Will.   By my advice,
Take all of them, for all are excellent.
If you would see a blind man, fix your eye
On yon Malvolio, blinded by conceit;
He mumbles greatness, greatness thrust on him.
If you would see an ass, there's Aguecheek:
A simple-minded, shallow nincompoop,
Full, full of emptiness.   If you would see
A man composed of jollity and drink,
There's Uncle Toby.   Scrutinize him well:
Those merry little eyes, that countenance
So rarely rubicund, that spacious belly,
And the rich splutter of his gurgling speech
Proclaim a constellation most adept
In midnight revel and symposium.
If you delight in shrewd diplomacy,

Observe Maria, how she deftly casts
Her angling-hook, and for no less a fish
Than big Sir Toby.   And if you delight
To bandy words, accost yon shaven fellow
In motley coat, with cap and bells ; I warrant
He knows a thing or two.   The pretty page
Hard by Orsino's side is Viola :
Love on her lips and patience in her eyes,
She is content to look on what she loves,
Until her harvest ripes, and she may feed
To her rich heart's content.

XIV.

List to the jingle now : a war of wit,
A wilderness of puns and repartee
And jibes and mockery.   Four merry maids
And each one mated to a goodly man,
Though perjured.   For these fellows had for-
        sworn
Female society.   Love's Labour's Lost
Is writ across their banner.   On they pass.

XV.

What may this creature be ; or beast or man,
That dashes towards us with impetuous haste
Alone and solitary?   Stop your ears !
The foulest pool in hell is sweet compared

To Timon's filthy mouth.   Here might the devil
Himself play pupil in vocabularies
And learn new oaths: for Timon's trumpet tongue
Leaves not a curse unuttered.   Foul and naked
He shakes his arms aloft and raves against
His fellow man. — This wretch, so needy now,
That from the earth he digs the sustaining root,
Was once endowed with opulence of gold
Like unto Crœsus.   Timon, look within !
'Tis not ingratitude of other men
That crumbled you.   You sinned 'gainst prop-
    erty,
Although it was your own, and now your deed
Falls heavily upon you.   Let us learn ;
There's a divinity in our possessions,
Which smites the offending prodigal as well
As him that hoards it.

XVI.

I hear the footfall of Homeric men,
I see the women of a classic age.
These fair proportions are not tailor-fathered :
The simple folds are beautiful because
The body swells symmetrical within,
Giving the garment life.   Here comes Aeneas
With mighty Hector, and that goodly pair
Is Troilus, constant both in love and war,
With his young brother, Paris; face and
    features

Seductive, proud and graceful as a god.
Peruse him well, that you may understand
Why Helen slipped.   Here is the king of men,
High Agamemnon, with his Spartan brother;
The brawny Ajax, fiery Diomed;
And yonder sullen man whose grim aspect
Threats thunder, that's Achilles in his wrath;
The type heroical that knows no law
But his own will.   First person singular
Is deity to him, and yet he smites
Those that would pray like he.   A tragic fate
Is thine, Achilles.   Nestor pleads with him,
But he attends not.   At his other side,
Behold Ulysses : lofty and serene
He steps 'mong men in proud pre-eminence,
For Jupiter on the Olympean peak
Is not more conscious of supremacy
Than this Ulysses.   In that massy brain,
Whose front is furrowed deep with meditation,
Pallas Athene keeps her laboratory,
Fusing the chaos of contending wills
To order infinite.— "But where is Helen?"
Nay, rest your eyes on him we speak of now,
None greater can be seen.   Our master poet
Speaks with a thousand tongues, but not a voice
From his immortal six and thirty plays
Comes laden with such pure philosophy,
Such unfringed logic, as the heavenly bard
Breathes with Ulysses lips.— "Now as I live,
That's Helen."   No, 'tis Cressida, false Cressid,

In whom the flush of roseate desire
Burns with an impure flame. She made her lips
A common pasture for the liberal Greeks
Ere yet the kisses of her Trojan lover
Had quit their fruitful print. A spotted soul
Widely inhabits the delicious body
Of foul-fair Cressida. See, how she plays
For Diomedes now: her breath is warm,
And Diomed will melt. She is a siren
Whose beauty is her chattels, and she doles them
Enticingly; uncovering here and there,
Now more, now less, e'en as the occasion
      prompts
To tempt the buyer.— "Tell me, where is
      Helen?"
Helen is here, but I'll not point her out,
Since many a man gazing upon this wonder
Did ever after seal his eyelids up,
Wishing to see no more.

XVII.

            The march goes on,
The Greeks and Trojans vanish from the scene,
Which now must shift from the Dardanean shore
To Rome eternal. Here's Coriolanus,
The proud patrician, and his Roman mother,
Volumnia, who loved her country more
Than all the world beside. For sacred Rome

She sacrificed her son, her valiant Caius,
Although no mother ever suckled child
So Titan-like as this one.   Mark the fall:
His pride was pardonable while his valor
In Rome's defense bepainted his fair body
With wounds as numerable as the stars
That shine in heaven's face; but when his pride,
For pride's sake only, jumped his spleeny hand
To slap the face of Rome — then he must die.
For Rome could never yet endure a man
Prouder than Rome.

XVIII.

The next that here appears
In Romish toga clad is not more tall
And not more heavy than the average Roman,
Yet when he stirred, the sides of the earth did
      spread
To furnish room and breathing space enough
For Julius Cæsar.   Nor before, nor since,
Have mighty and diverging faculties
In any one man so been multiplied
As in this Cæsar.   On his right hand walks
The festive Antony, whom soon we'll see
Spurning the sway and sceptre of the world
To melt in Egypt's arms.—There is the faction:
Keen and sagacious Cassius ; Marcus Brutus,
Less wise than honorable ; plain blunt Casca

With Cinna, Decius, and the entire band
Of high conspirators, who could not see
That Cæsar's spirit was a mightier thing
Than Cæsar's flesh.   Now will Marc Antony,
Possessed with Julius' disembodied soul,
Set Rome ablaze, and on Philippi field
Will Cæsar's ghost grasp the great traitor's
      sword
And stick 't in's traitor heart.

XIX.

                              Behold, a ship!
It hails from Afric's shore, from Egypt's sum-
      mer,
Where the warm god who teems in Nilus' banks
Kisses the foot of Alexandria's wall
With fruitful lips.   This paraphernal vision,
Which looms on 's like a dream of the Orient,
Is Cleopatra's sloop divinely rigged
Against the one-third owner of the earth.
The battles met on Cydnus' swelling waters,
Marc Antony assailed the Amazon,
Boarded her vessel, looked upon his foe —
And fell.   See, where the deck is super-roofed
With tasseled canopy and silken curtain
To gainsay entrance to Apollo's eye,
There did Antonius offer up a crown
On Venus' altar : there his empire melts.

On cushions and on skins of lionesses
He lies o'erwhelmed with Egypt's amorous
    queen;
And what keen steel, plots and advantages,
Rome's surfeit and starvation on the Alps
Could never scratch, lies here unmanned and
    drowned
In a stagnant pool. Rome's mightiest reveler
Is here outwassailed, and the glorious trunk
That rose in battle like a second Mars
Now tumbles on an Alexandrian couch,
Whose rare calidity and orient breath
Makes death demandable.—But reasoning Rome
Can never wear the Eastern manacles,
And therefore breeds a worthier, wiser son,
Octavius Cæsar. All the winds of the South
Exhale their soft indulgencies in vain
On rigid Cæsar. Rome's triumvirate crown
He'll beat to a single circle wide as the earth,
And wear 't alone.

XX.

Now lapse a thousand years. On Saxon soil
These nobles played their part. Here comes
    King John,
Who ruled o'er England hard upon the time
That Cœur-de-Lion with chivalric arm
Essayed to wrest the sepulchre of Christ

From Saracenic dogs. But this King John,
Who held his sceptre by the nation's choice,
A charter loftier than a lineal throne,
Grew much unworthy: for he killed Prince
    Arthur,
The lineal heir, deeming him dangerous,
Albeit himself sat on high England's throne,
A people-chosen monarch. So he drops
In the shears of contradiction. Note, I pray,
You clean-faced man. Him the Pope Innocent
Employed as legate from the see of Rome
To toy and tool with kingdoms. For it chanced
That in those days our mother church waxed
    warm
With secular affection, and her love
To compass worldly passion, stripped her body
Of the celestial robes. Now fortune's winds
Will blow her round and round, and she must
    take
Her chances with a host of temporal powers,
Shuffling for good or ill. Following after
Come Philip, King of France, Louis, the Dau-
    phin,
And the Archduke of Austria. These attempted
With their conjointed armies and intrigues
To fix a foreign foot on Britain's soil,
A deed incompassable. Here's the man
Calls conquest folly. That is Faulconbridge,
The hero national, the lion whelp
Of lion-hearted Richard. All his life

Is life for England. On the chalky cliffs
That beetle o'er the channel, he will sit
And roar his warning thunder to the world,
Beware, for I am England.

XXI.

Still they come!
Another king, another royal troop:
Richard the Second. Listen to the names
Of those that follow: Henry Bolingbroke,
The Duke of Hereford, and Richard's cousin;
Old John of Gaunt, the Duke of Lancaster;
The Dukes of Norfolk, Surrey and of York;
Salisbury, and the Earl Northumberland
With his son Harry Percy, Hotspur called,
Whom in the next troop we shall meet again.—
King Richard, willful and extravagant,
Reigned without scruple; ignorant of the fact,
That any man to be a nation's king
Must be the nation's servant. High and low
He tyrannized and trampled; robbed the people,
And levied on the lands and movables
Of the nobility. He banished Hereford,
And went a-romping on an Irish war.
But mark the harvest: Henry Bolingbroke,
Allied with other nobles wronged by Richard,
Returns to England, lands at Ravensburg
In Gloucestershire, and wheresoe'er he goes

The people clap him. Henry's rising star
Mounts high in England's heaven. Troop on
    troop
Flocks to his banner, and all hail him king.
The wily and far-reaching politician
Knew how to win men's hearts. Then poor
    King Richard
By all forsaken, yields his royalty,
And Bolingbroke is crowned King Henry Fourth.
In Pomfret Castle Richard met his end
At hands directed by his cousin king. —
No doubt, his faults were great ones and were
    many ;
Still, we do love the lone-in-prison monarch
When like a cagéd bird he sings of death:
Our motion weakens, and our phantasy
Dwells in the gloomy tower there with Richard
Chanting of dirges with the poet king.

XXII.

Give me a cup of sack! O star of Eastcheap,
Rise once again and let thy twinkling eye
Spark merrily, for the prosaic world
Burns smoky-wet. This is, indeed our Jack,
Our monster Jack, our Jack of jest and swagger,
Our drinking, laughing, lying, plump old Jack,
With whom to spend a day is worth a year.
The rogues of Gadshill and the Boarshead
    tavern,

Like satellites encircling their sun,
Attend on Falstaff.   There's the bombast Pistol,
Hack, whack and crack.   Peto and Poins, I spy.
That's Bardolph, with the jack-o'-lantern nose;
And yon fair stripling prodding Falstaff's ribs
Is Harry Monmouth, Prince of Wales, hereafter
Wielding the scepter as King Henry Fifth.
But while he swims with these unsavory fish
We call him Hal.   Sir John delights the prince,
And Hal adores the man in whose construction
The beastliest belly and the rarest wit
Crossed like the web the woof.   And but that
        we
Must see the rest, we would along with them,
For, look you, Falstaff's jelly paunch 'gins
        tremble
In premonition of a laboring jest. —
Here come the nobles whose assisting hands
Holp Bolingbroke to mount the English throne;
And now they see his love for them abating
E'en with his need of them.   Hence they con-
        spire
To pluck the upstart down; but Henry's power,
Which lives encysted in the hearts o' the people
Bears down the rebels. — On a field of Mars,
Near Shrewsbury, the fiery Hotspur met
With Henry Monmouth.   From the London
        slums
This young Apollo mounts the vaulted sky,
Straining for Percy's star.   The battles meet,

And lo! the meteor flashes into night,
Eclipsed by Henry's sun.

XXIII.

Our Jack appears once more, our only Jack,
Our prince of jest and frolic. What's the
    matter,
That with a mien discomfited and sad
He sneaks apart, the butt of all men's laughter?
He needed money, man ; and on the way
His carnal appetite o'ertook his wit.
And now such ordinary men as Page
And Ford, at Windsor with their merry wives
With safe impunity make sport of him,
Who, ere he fell, defied the entire world
To engage with him in the tilting-yard of wit,
And there cross arms.

XXIV.

Now comes the time when Henry crowned the
    Fifth
Contemplates what to do. From the high seat
Where fortune and his merit have upreared him
He casts his kingly eye o'er his possessions,
And wheresoe'er he looks, he looks on peace.
Rebellion is put down, and fruitful labor,
Which maketh one man's gain another's profit,

Breeds amity in all. The soldier only
Bewails his occupation, and with Henry
Yawns at the idle years. — Whene'er the strong
Seek quarrel with the weak, 'tis never long
Before some friend pricked by ulterior aims
Shows facile ground; as in the present case
The Archbishop of Canterbury shows
To eager Henry. " France, my liege, is yours,
And by the true law of inheritance
Your head should wear it's crown."   The wily
    prelate,
Like tempting Satan with our mother Eve,
Pours his persuasion into willing ears;
For Henry answers, " If then France be ours,
We owe it both to heaven and our honor
To bend or break it."— Look, there comes the
    king
From Harfleur with all England at his heels,
Flouting the French air with his British flags.
Behold the wildering maze of pike and lance,
Which like a forest looms upon our sight;
Behold the archers and artillery,
The serried footmen and the myriad horse
Beating their martial rhythm on the soil
Of trembling France. The mighty mass moves
    on,
Shaking the air as when a hurricane
Moans in the distant wood. Scabbard and steel,
Helmet, plate, armor, and habiliments
And creaking saddles shuffle in the press

That sweeps on Agincourt.— King Henry con-
    quers,
And while he lives, like to a second giant
Of Rhodus' fame, he plants one foot in England,
And wears the other on the neck of France.

XXV.

If sons are punished for their father's guilt,
See, how the wheeling Nemesis alights
On infant Henry's head, Henry the Sixth.
And now the day of glory sinks in night,
The pride of conquest into sad defeat;
What Henry stole, from Henry shall be stolen,
And lawless gain shall be a lawful loss.
So retribution sings and sweeps adown
To pack the deeds of men upon their back.—
The maid of Orleans with the aid of heaven
Slips England's yoke from the fair neck of
    France,
Discomfiting the Britains; who now home,
Begin to quarrel on whose fault it was
That France escaped them. In the Temple
    Garden
The hot nobility of England splits
In rival faction. York and Lancaster
Assumed the white and red rose as an emblem,
When quickly all the park was stripped of roses
Arrayed in colory difference on the front

Of spleeny partisans.— For twenty years
These fiends incarnate butchered one another
Decked in the signs of love and innocence,
The symbols that God's blessed angels wear,
Roses of white and red. — These are not men
That pass us by, but the unbodied wraiths
Of those who fell upon a hundred fields,
Were stabbed in prison, strangled in their beds,
Drowned, poisoned or secreted unto death
In hungry cells.   How like a phantom flight
Of paly ghosts they seem.   Hover away,
Weird apparition!   Though dame History
Remembers many of these wounded spirits,
. Let us not name them ; only, pray you, mark
You crookback fellow perched upon his charger
Like a mal-shapen ape.   That's Richard Gloster,
Whose blast infernal swept the blushing rose
Of Henry's faction to the scattering wind;
Which done, this hell-worm clapped his venom
        teeth
Into the petals of the milk-white rose,
The rose of York, the much abuséd symbol
Of his own house — but we anticipate
Events yet unaccrued.

XXVI.

Oft in a wet-warm summer you have seen
Some garden smothered in obnoxious weeds
Ugly to sight and smell.   Anon a gardener

Enters the gate, a weed hook in his hand,
To extirpate the rank offensive weeds
That grew sans invitation.   Eagerly
He plucks and pulls and spares no gross usurper,
Albeit some tender flowret, too, must perish
For having twined its rootlets all too near
Some noisome creature that is doomed for good.
So ever even justice 'gins to work
In England's garden. — Richard is her tool,
Who pricked with sharp ambition for the crown
'Complished her purpose well.   Look, where he
      comes,
The dark, unconscious minister of fate,
And 'hind him all the harvest of his edge,
Cropped, as he wist it, in his own behalf.
There goes King Henry, of his name the sixth,
And his son Edward, both by Gloster slain,
In London Tower and at Tewksbury.
Next   follow   Edward   Fourth   and   perjured
      Clarence,
Brothers and obstacles to rising Richard;
And next the lords of Rivers, Vaughan, Grey,
Who fell in Pomfret Castle.   Yon is Hastings,
Who jubilating o'er his rivals' end,
Little expected that the lord protector
Would this day swear by Paul, he'd never eat
Till Hastings' head were off.   That's Bucking-
      ham,
A villain, but not deeply died enough
To please the bloody Richard.   So, in time,

He too is tumbled.   See, the women there ;
York's aged duchess, type of tragic. woe,
For she is Richard's mother, and men call her
The devil's dam.   Peer closely in the press,
And you will see three bands of glittering gold
Circling the foreheads of three widowed queens:
Of Margaret, Elizabeth and Anne,
The one-time wives of Henry and two Edwards.—
O England, droop not, bear thee bravely up:
The day will come, albeit the night is long.
E'en now I see a glimmering in the South,
Where Richmond, hovering o'er the sea from
          France,
Breaks like the dawn on Britain's tearful gloom.
Come now to Bosworth, once more let us look
Upon the fiend there writhing in the hell
Of his own conscience.   See him toss and groan
In frightful slumber, leaping out of bed,
Trembling with icy drops upon his brow,
Crying, Have mercy, Jesu.— Even then
The man who said, I am myself alone,
Was overcome by seeing what he was. —
His body fell on Bosworth bloody field,
But Richard never was himself again
After he saw his image in the glass
Of that horrific dream.

XXVII.

The last we shall behold of England's kings,
Henry the Eighth: gross and libidinous,
Devoid of honor and replete in senses,
A six-wived monster. Still the wise Creator
Wrought nought for nothing. And, indeed, this
    Henry,
Like to Mephisto in the Goethean Faust,
Ruled over men as portion of that power
Which always wills the bad but works the good.
Small care had he that men should be enlight-
    ened,
And yet he trimmed the lamp of Reformation
With much success. He wived not with Ann
    Boleyn
Because his conscience flamed for her religion
With warmer zeal than for the Roman faith
Of Catholic Katherine; and yet, 'twas he
By whose device a most illustrious queen
Cried mother to Ann Boleyn. 'Twas not love
For Thomas Cranmer as a Lutheran
That made him Archbishop of Canterbury,
But rather for he holp his giddy king
To browse in greener pasture. That is Cranmer
With whom the king there whispers as they walk;
A learned man and wise, whose aim in life
Was ever to do well. Two women follow
The queens of Henry, Katherine and Anne.

See, what a tale of woe and misery
Misfortune wrote upon the pale complexion
Of Katherine's cheek.   She was a loyal queen,
A wife most patient, and a woman gifted
With a degree of gentle dignity,
As leaves us ever in a pleasing doubt
Twixt love and admiration.   For Anne Boleyn,
King Henry said, " She is a dainty one,"
And so you see she is.   But trust not beauty:
It raised Anne Boleyn to the bed of England,
And from that dizzy steep it cast her stumbling
Down to the headsman's block.— Look, there is
      Wolsey,
The crafty prelate, Lord High Chancellor
And Cardinal of York.   He looked towards
      Rome,
And in his mighty greed malfeased the trust
Of double office to unholy uses.
But Wolsey never sat in Peter's chair;
He fell dishonored, and in Leicester Abbey
He penitently died.   The nation prospered,
And from the life of this ambitious man,
Doubled by church and state, she made con-
      clusion,
That never hence a cardinal should be
Prime minister of England.

XXVIII.

The quarried monument whose sepulchre
Immures the ancient dust of Capulet,
Now yields his treasure; and the ponderous gates
Yawn on their sleepy and slow moving hinges,
That Juliet and her Romeo may come forth
To grace our triumph. We may truly call
These lovers wretched, for an adverse fate
Denied to them their one and single joy.
But who is happy, if it be not they
That feed upon a passion, which omitted
Makes life and the whole earth to live it in
A thing detested?   Never did grim death
Accept an invitation that was tendered
So cheerfully as this. — Verona's night
No longer burns these torches in her brow;
The stars are fallen and their fire quenched.

XXIX.

Robed in silks
Of primal hue, in raiment all bedashed
With emerald and far-gleaming chrysolite,
Behold, the Moor of Venice, black Othello,
The valiant savior of the watery town.
What can the state deny to him that saves it?
Therefore the duke and summoned dignitaries,
To grace their warrior, needs must sanctify

His dusky marriage to the whitest dove
That flutters in all Venice. Confidently
The timid bird aspires to mate the eagle
Who soars pre-eminent above all men
Of her complexion; and she loves the hero,
Although a sooty bosom hides his heart.
But nature, for some reason wise or foolish,
Sets down prescription: to maintain the race
She immolates the individual,
That leaps beyond the barrier. Desdemona
Offends the ethics of morality,
Assaults the family, hence the family's honor
Justly demands her death. Inferior things
Trust not the finer that descend to them;
Hence the world-spirit brings Iago forth
(A lesser wit had served the cause as well)
To inoculate the inexperienced Moor
With jealousy. How could Othello trust,
When Desdemona's honor to her husband
Dishonored her?

XXX.

King Lear, Cordelia, Regan, Goneril,
Kent, Gloster, Edmund, Edgar and the Fool.
If ever vice and virtue measured arms,
If ever man was overcome with error,
If ever evil came to evil end
And merit ever made its owner happy, —
Then look on these. Observe the human act

Seeking its proper level in the scales
Of divine compensation. Doting Lear,
The monarch absolute whose law is will,
And will, caprice, strips his authority,
Spurns the one prop whereon his title rests,
And wonders why he falls. There comes Cor-
    delia:
In proud humility she frets her father,
Accepts her banishment, and linked with France
Seeks to restore her father. To which end
She leads an alien army o'er the channel
Against the British state. Cordelia dies.
Goneril and Regan plot against their father,
Against their husbands next, and true to nature,
Devour each other. Gloster slipped in wedlock,
And as the wheel goes round, the bastard worm
Bites the offending parent. Edmund Gloster
Wreaks woeful vengeance on the institution
That cast him out. He smites the family,
Until his deeds of darkness come to light —
Then smites himself.— King Lear's capricious
    rule
Breeds baneful vapors in the British court:
The sultry air stifles the breath of man,
Till passion bursts the ponderous atmosphere
With deafening thunder. Curses cry to heaven,
And retribution shrieks. Fate's fiery bolt
Rives top to bottom, singeing high and low.
And when the purgéd air is sweet and wholesome,
Behold, we see the Fool and Kent and Edgar,

Wisdom and charity and innocence,
Survive the tempest of contending ills ;
Their qualities are blessèd.

XXXI.

In rugged Scotland, Duncan's feeble rule
Fostered sedition, and his impotence
Invoked the Norse and Dane to land their powers
In quest of spoil and venture.   Not so fast.
Here comes a subject mightier than his king,
Macbeth, puissant.   Neither foe nor rebel
Can grow in Scotland while great Glamis' arm
Strikes for his country.   On the western coast
He quells MacDonald and his lawless band
Of Kernes and Gallowglasses ; in the East
He whips the invaders from the shores of Fife
With sword invincible.   The battles won,
Our conquering hero turns his horse's head
Towards Inverness.   Alas, that it should be,
But thus it is, success begets temptation.
And so the while his fiery mettled steed
Paces o'er moor and fen and Scottish heath,
Macbeth in salient rumination wrapt
Sees the weird sisters, whose prophetic crown
Gleams in his fevery vision like the star
That shone o'er Bethlehem.   He gallops home,
And when the wedded partner of his bosom
Throbbed in his arms, he felt ambition's flames

Raging in her heart, too.— The deed is done —
Duncan is slain. Now, Macbeth, kill thyself,
For both ways thou must die.   If thou art traitor,
Then rip thy bowels with the self-same steel
That minced Mac Donald : if thou art a king,
Then plunge the sleeping dagger in thy breast
That stabbed King Duncan.   Thou hast cast thy
    life
Between the opposing millstones of thy acts,
No god can save thee.— Hecate now appears
Soothing his terror with security.
The foul witch lies; but that's the good of evil,
And therefore still the devil holds his office,
To pinch the proselyte whom first he tempts.

XXXII.

These are the actors from the tragic scene
That played in Elsinore.   The moody prince,
Within whose gentle bosom thought and deed,
Dwelt like two strangers. Next the bloody
    uncle
And the salacious queen, who can not pray,
Because they still persist to feed upon
The fruits of their offense.   Yon ancient man,
Who talks and talks and talks, that is Polonius,
An over-anxious creature of the king,
Whose cunning ran to seed.   Behind him follow
More of the ilk would pit their nut-shell brain

'Gainst Hamlet's intellect. They might as well
Bail the salt ocean with their hollow hand.
The mice would play with the cat; pray, mark
    the sport,
For since the day intriguery began
Was never knave so lamentably beaten,
As these, our Rosencrantz and Guildenstern.—
There goes Laertes eager to avenge
His father's murder. To his hasty arm
The frail Ophelia clings. She loved Prince Ham-
    let,
And truly he loved her. But she was weak :
Her all mistrusting father, and her brother,
With lungs still reeking with the fumes of Paris,
Made her believe, that Hamlet's protestations
Were but the hot and hungry ministers
Of fleshly appetite.—But Hamlet, Hamlet,
What shall we say of thee? Not one of us
But wears an umbrage of thy life's collision
In his own bosom. By the grace of God,
We share with Him the faculty of reason,
And rise exalted o'er creation else,
To be his image. But this godlike reason
So trembles twixt intelligence and will,
That oft we lose our balance. — Think and do,
Sums all philosophy. Now, as to Hamlet,
His deeds were still-born, strangled in their birth
By infinite conjecture, speculation,
And spinning out of possibilities,
What might befall if this or that were done,

And so the end is nothing. Circumstances,
He lacks the will to shape, now shape his ends,
And then he throws intelligence aside,
And swears by fate: " The providence is all,
What comes will come," and so he runs to death
With eyes wide open. First he thinks and acts
  not,
And then he acts and thinks not. Hark, a drum !
Young Fortinbras, a man of head and hand,
Is come to rule in Denmark. Hamlet died,
But his Horatio lived to tell the story,
Reporting Hamlet and his cause aright
To the unsatisfied.

POEMS.

A Wanderer.

Over the land I pass,
   Over the sea,
Roaming about, about,
   Aimlessly.

All the wide North and South,
   East and the West,
Equally furnish me
   Room for my rest.

One time there was spot,
   Dearer to me
Than all the earth beside
   Ever can be.

Life is a mystic thing;
   Fire and frost:
Love is so easily won,
   Easily lost.

(47)

Over the land I pass,
  Over the sea,
Roaming about, about,
  Aimlessly.

Into the gates of Rome,
  Listless I drift;
Into the gloomy past,
  Shadows to lift.

Over the forum there
  Glances the moon;
Images rise around,
  But, ah, too soon

Voices and feet I hear
  Passing near by;
Others have come to see,
  Even as I.

Jolly good folk are they,
  Hear, how they laugh;
Here on an age's tomb
  Merrily chaff.

Wondrous coincidence!
  Moon, disappear!
Now I am recognized,
  Now she is here.

Lightly she speaks to me —
  Angel of hell —
" How do you do, my friend?"
  Thank you, well, well.

My Choice.

If I could choose, I would not be
A soldier who o'er land and sea
Bears high command, whose simple breath
Brings unto hundreds life and death.

If I could choose, I would not be
A statesman, though of high degree ;
For rarely can the people know
If your design be high or low.

If I could choose, I would not be
A connoisseur whose eulogy
Flows like his wine with fowl and fish;
As if the world swam in his dish.

If I could choose, I would not be
An upper-tendom votary,
To lounge in silk with painted faces
And shallow skulls in fashion's places.

If I could choose, I would not be
A rich man, for it seems to me

4

A fellow were a foolish lout
To carry in and carry out.

If I could choose, then it should be
A little cottage by the sea,
Or by the lake, or laughing brook,
But it should be a quiet nook.

Far from the city it should be,
With hills and hollow, wood and lea;
And twenty acres should be found
For tillage and for pasture ground.

And in my little home need be
No bric-a-brac, no tapestry,
No plated stove, no bronzed clocks,
Nor marble basins with silvered cocks.

But in this home of mine should be
Besides things of necessity,
Some twenty books, some tools to write,
And logs to burn in winter night.

Man's wish is boundless, but you see
With me 'tis all reality:
The field, the farm, the wood, the brook,
The house, the chimney and the book.

The reason why all things to me
Have come so bountiful and free,

Is built upon the simple plan
To merely wish for what I can.

Now let us in, and you shall see
The spirit that attends on me;
The nimble fingers, lips and laugh,
That double all by claiming half.

Her Birthday.

(December 31st.)

"The end shall crown the rest," said Father
    Time,
But how excel the joy which every day
Of the now closing year stands blessed withal?
One circle of the sun alone remained,
When Kronos whispered into Cupid's ear:
"Grapple thy wings, sweet Cupid, fly apace
O'er sun and moon to every bright-eyed star,
And whatsoever fairest meets thine eye,
Bring it to yonder little darkling spot
That man inhabits." — Cupid, in a flash,
Clapped bow and quiver on his dimpled shoulder,
Slipped from Olympus, swept the universe —
And ere the day had ended thou wert born. —
And now, methinks, I see a long procession
Of spring and summer and of autumn days
With envious eye look on their wintry sister,
The last and youngest daughter of the year,

Who wears so bright a jewel.   Is it strange,
The next day should begin another year?
What could the old do more?

My Dream and Helen's.

After the noon of a summer day
While in a drowsy hammock I lay,
Reason took leave, and fancy took wing,
With franchise becoming a heavenly thing.

Sultry the air, and its thermal stream
Lazily sighed in a tropical gleam,
Whelmed me so willingly, more and more,
Waved me and washed me on dreamland's shore.

There in a fairyland wondrous cool,
Roving in moonlight by placid pool,
Helen I met, for the dream-god's play
Laughs at the trammels of earth and day.

Washed in the beams of the watery star
Helen is pale, and her beauty at war:
Forehead and cheek in their wan fellowship
Challenge the flush of her scarlet lip.

Helen and I own but half a heart,
Which the nice world keeps forever apart.
Here we are free: 'tis no earthly harm,
But heaven's delight to link arm in arm.

Silent are we, and silent the wood,
Silence the language so well understood:
Softly we loiter by rill and well,
Pine needle forest and mossy dell.

Never in life were the forests so green;
Never in life were such landscapes seen:
Castles of marble with turrets of gold,
Gardens and fountains and statues untold.

Helen is mine, for her melting eye
Grants me the prayer which the gods would deny:
Here I may revel in rapturous bliss,
Drinking the fire of Helen's kiss.—

What! have really I been sleeping?
Six o'clock! I shall be late;
Five o'clock 's the time appointed,
And by this, I know they wait.

See, we have a class in Homer;
Once a week we join to read
Homer's wars and Homer's legend,
Singing of the mighty deed.

And to-day I would not miss it,
Helen is our gentle host;
Whence with several bright companions
We embark for Ilium's coast.

So with drops of cooling water
I dispel my summer dream ;
Put my Homer in my pocket,
Hie me quickly to the scene.

But the bard is dull this evening,
Wise Athené veils her look ;
And the lesson hurried over,
I am glad to close the book.

Ask me not why Hector perished,
Why Ulysses doubts and seems :
Let us change the subject-matter,
Tell me, what you think of dreams?

Dreams are nonsense, Helen answers;
I detest the shadowy crew:
I have dreamt as clear as noonday
What I know was never true.

So have I — the words escape me
Much too slowly, much too soon;
For her cheek assumed the pallor
Which it wore this afternoon.

Which ?

Shall it be eyes in eyes, or lips on lips?
I cannot tell which were the greater bliss;
Therefore your eyes shall be my volume's pages,
And for the period, lips shall print a kiss.

Too Late.

My neighbor's garden yonder
  Is rich beyond compare,
For in it blooms a flower,
  A sweet rose, passing fair.

It grew not there by nature;
  A little year ago
I saw it in the meadow,
  Where myriad blossoms blow.

And often, just for pastime,
  I strolled across the lane;
The rose was glad to see me,
  And I went on again.

My neighbor, worldly wiser,
  He boldly dug it out
And set it in his garden,
  With hedges round about.

I, too, had leave to take it,
  And own it if I chose:
I never knew how sorely
  My life would miss this rose.

And daily now I wander
  Before my neighbor's gate,

And look upon the treasure
Which I esteemed too late.

The southwind gently whispers;
I drink the fragrant breath,
Which might have been my heaven,
And now is almost death.

She knows her tardy lover,
She turns and smiles on me;
And in her blushing countenance
A touch of pain I see.

The Children's Ball.

Music peals and laughter mingles,
Silks and satin float before;
Gentle men and gentle-women
Here are met on fashion's floor.

What a merry, noisy bustle
Fills the bright illumined hall;
Bells and beaux of tiny stature,
For to-night is children's ball.

In the maze of little dancers
One wee maiden holds my eye,
Mouth and nose and step and gesture —
Irony of fate, oh why!

Well I know that where the lamb is
    I shall also find the ewe,
So I walk through arch and gallery —
    There she is, her husband, too.

" Glad to see you well," he greets me,
    " Just the man I'm looking for;
Entertain my wife, old fellow,
    There's a friend out at the door."

Grow we all so dull indifferent?
    Off he goes, and now are we,
She and I alone, together,
    Left each other's company.

Think not, that such fair occasion
    Could our ancient fire renew :
We are gentle folk and therefore
    All extravagance eschew.

Nay, we criticised the people,
    Cut of beard, and cut of gown,
Politics and education,
    And the topics of the town.

On the weather we commented,
    Summer's heat and winter's cold,
That the ball was well attended,
    And enjoyed by young and old.

As we looked at one another,
　　Was it sinful, that within
Fancy built a fairy palace
　　In the realm of might have been?

Conversation, filmy nothing,
　　Faded into silent thought;
Thoughts of many a dear encounter
　　By our heart's deep passion wrought.

There the hand and there the fingers
　　That so often crept in mine,
Interlacing and caressing,
　　Hungry with the flame divine.

There the lips, my lips she called them
　　Once — but see, her fringéd lid
Opens wide, our eyes have entered,
　　And the tears start forth unbid.

And we do not wish to check them,
　　Sorrow, too, may claim a right,
But the place — a quivering whisper,
　　" Fare thee well, good night, good night!"

Music peals and laughter mingles,
　　Silks and satin float before;
And the world runs on forever,
　　And a voice cries, weep no more.

My Rose.

What strange emotion racks my breast?
　　Why do I shun the sight
Of city, country, friend and book?
　　Why do I shun the light?

I saw my rose, my rose, to-night,
　　The rose of my summer day;
I had not seen her, oh so long,
　　And summer had flown away.

In the pride of her youth my rose was plucked,
　　Plucked for a bride to be,
Plucked by the hand of a good, brave man,
　　Pity, oh, pity me!

I tried to forget and I had forgot
　　Our passion and our glee:
I had forgot how I loved this rose,
　　Forgot how the rose loved me.

I saw my rose again to-night,
　　She said — I do not know —
But on her lips and eyes I traced
　　Memories of long ago.

And now the storm wells up anew,
　　The tempest rives my soul,

I lock me in my lonely cell,
  And from the distant goal

My summer rose, my summer love,
  My rose of halcyon May,
Blooms forth afresh, uncharms the spell :
  The past becomes to-day.

I clasp her to my yearning heart,
  The body and the soul:
Oh, I could weep my spirit out!
  All, nothing, severed, whole!

I press my head in the pillowed down,
  I shroud me in my sheet :
The spell will pass ; aye, so will I ;
  Could we but passing meet.

Defiance.

This little life of ours
  Lives like a spark,
Flashes ephemeral,
  Sinks in the dark.

Brief is the passionate
  Love in our breast ;
Death makes an end of it,
  Puts it to rest.

Soon shall thy raven locks,
    Forehead of snow,
Cheeks of the rose's blush,
    Yield to the foe.

Soon shall thy bosom deep
    Rise not nor fall:
Cold, all its fire quenched,
    Motionless all.

Soon thy warm crimson lip
    Breathing desire,
Soon shall thy gleaming eye
    Flashing love's fire,

Deep in the earth be laid,
    There to decay,
Into the elements
    Passing away.

Had we but met in time
    All had been well;
Now a mere whim of chance
    Dooms us to hell.

Conscience, we challenge thee,
    Conscience, we dare!
Man's poor formalities
    Vanish in air.

Mortals may promise, but
   Fate rules the man,
And irresistibly
   Forces her plan.

Now is eternity,
   Future and Past:
Living, we live but once,
   Nothing can last.

Now is love's only time,
   Now we are here.
Why do we hesitate?
   What do we fear?

Let me encompass thee,
   Moment of bliss;
Let me thus clasping thee
   Die with a kiss!

Die with my lips on thine,
   Drinking thy breath!
Moment of ecstacy!
   Welcome, O death!

Resignation.

Though thine eyes' mystery
　Softly assures,
Telling me, yieldingly,
　Take me, I'm yours :

Though thy warm clinging hand
　Thrills me and tells,
Love's eager willingness
　Rises and swells,

Throbs in my arteries,
　Pulses divine !
Ecstacy infinite !
　Take me, I'm thine :

Though from thy parted lips
　Amorous breath
Fans my ambition, till
　Fearless of death :

Though from thy lips I drink
　Kisses like wine,
Kisses, that pray to me,
　Come and be mine :

Still I must banish thee,
　Helen, adieu !

Love must be sacrificed,
　　Life must be true;

True to the vows we made.
　　Curséd the fate,
That our stars' orbits cross
　　Useless, too late!

Resolute, resolute,
　　Helen, farewell!
Far, in the realm beyond
　　All will be well.

There without fear or shame,
　　Passionate, warm,
Lie everlastingly
　　Locked in my arm.

In Love's Remembrance.

The village sleeps, the time is night,
　　The belfry's tongue tells one, two, three:
There is no moon, and the wintry wind
　　Hangs frozen crystals on bush and tree.

But look, a light is burning still
　　In yonder window near the roof.
It is our ancient pedagogue
　　Searching the past for light and proof.

He is a bookworm, verily,
  This gray, lean, spectacled old man,
· Mousing in parchment and musty page,
  Forgetting life is but a span.

He climbs upon his creaky stool,
  And tugs at a book high up on the wall;
It tumbles in a cloud of dust,
  And from its leaves what treasures fall!

The old man stoops and gathers all
  In his withered hand. His back is old,
And rising, aches ; he hobbles on,
  And sits, his finding to unfold : —

Brittle leaves, a wilted rose-bud,
  Clover from a lucky spot,
And a faded silken ribbon
  With the words, forget-me-not.

Handkerchief, embroidered deftly
  With a magic monogram ;
Glove, by dance and moonlight stolen.
  Souls that in Elysium swam !

And a ringlet, sunny golden,
  Folded in a tinted sheet,
With a message, hundred kisses,
  Yes, to-night — but be discreet.

5

Morpheus comes and stoops the lover
 On his treasures, soft and low,
While his fine remembrance revels
 In the dreams of long ago.

.   .   .   .

The light still burns, albeit the sun
 Illumines shelves and books and bed.
A smile plays on the schoolman's lip ;
 The schoolman — he is dead.

To Shakespeare.

Henry and Hamlet,
 Born by chance,
Were raised to fame
 On Shakespeare's lance.

Supreme creator,
 Who of man,
Save our Redeemer
 Leads thy van :

The woe and weal
 Of great and small
Responded to
 Thy magic call.—

I learned to love,
 When yet a child,

Thy wondrous music
Fierce and mild :

With growing years,
I 'gan to see
The truth of thy
Philosophy.

Thy clarion voice
Rings from the goal,
Starting an echo
In my soul ;

And now I prattle
Of king and clown,
Of earth and heaven,
Up and down.

My truest notes
I owe to thee ;
The false to my
Infirmity.

Daphne's Song.

(From Telemachus.)

There was a great city beyond a great sea
Famous in war and in glory;
Priam was king, and a son had he,

As gay and as gallant as any could be :
  Paris, the prince of my story.

But Paris and prudence went ever astray,
  Cupid alone was his master:
He journeyed from Ilium to Sparta one day,
And stole Menelaus' fair Helen away,
  Heedless of any disaster.

No sooner had Paris with Helen set sail,
  Helen, the pride of her nation,
Than each mighty monarch put on his mail,
At Aulis they gathered in spite of a gale,
  Aulis, the ultimate station.

Nine winters and summers they battled in vain
  Wasting the fields of Scamander ;
A thousand brave heroes and horsemen were slain,
But none could the beautiful Helen regain.
  Tell me, was none to unhand her?

O yes, little Ithaca, isle of the sea,
  Hail to Ulysses' endeavor:
He captured the city and set Helen free,
A master of mighty invention was he.
  Praise him for aye and forever.

Kate's Song.

(From Sibyl.)

Summer ties his bundle up,
  He is doomed to wander ;
Balmy days and moonlit night
Packs he in his bundle tight,
  He will nothing squander.

Pansy and forget-me-not,
  Pink and rose and myrtle,
Bob-o'-link and whip-poor-will,
Fly with him o'er wood and hill.
  Hear the north-wind hurtle !

Lusty winter, clad in white,
  Captures field and city :
At the window snow and sleet ;
Down the chimney, in the street,
  Listen to his ditty.

Wool and fur shall keep us warm,
  Cheery glows the fire ;
And the singing kettle blows
Steam from out his iron nose —
  Pussy joins the choir.

Bring the fife and violin,
  Trip a dancing measure.

William, William, you may croak,
But to us, a jolly folk,
  Life is full of pleasure.

Summer, summer, fare thee well,
  Come again to-morrow.
Winter, winter, every year
You shall find a welcome here.
  Banish pain and sorrow.

Nil.

Man sees his aim, and mostly 'tis a good one;
But it lies anchored in a far, far sea.
He plunges in, divides the angry billows,
But while he nobly struggles on his way,
See, how the witching sirens, Love and Plenty,
Kiss all the brave ambition from his brow.
They sing and laugh and creep into his bosom;
He dallies with the means, forgoes the end.

Man.

Presumptuous man, and why shouldst thou be
    proud?
Walk to the wood and set thy six small feet
Against the lofty pine; or pit thy arms
Against the foam-capped breakers, when they lash

The rocky limit of their wide domain,
And where art thou? Nor can thy puny voice
O'ercrow the little span from tongue to ear,
When the great tempest winds his shrilly horn.
Thy eyes are dull compared to those bright eyes
That twinkle from the raven brow of night;
The joy of summer makes thy merriest laugh
A sickly smile; nor can thy weeping lids
Prevail against the copious tears of heaven.
Stoop, mortal, stoop! you crawl upon the earth
Ten thousand years; you dig and build and sweat,
But all in vain; your proudest monument,
Set at the base of towering Himalay,
Shows like a wart. — Be humble, say no more,
And walk in lowly silence to thy grave.—
No, not a wit! I am the lord of all.
I tread the earth triumphant under foot,
For she is mine, my primal heritage.
Why should I tremble at the elements
When they are bondmen to my intellect,
Which holds them as it were in prenticeship
To serve my uses? When they mutiny,
I summon one in arms to curb the other.
My realm is all in all; for earth and fire,
The wind, the wave, the wood, sun, stars and
    moon
Must furnish tribute for my benefit.
The boisterous wind and the big surgy sea
Propel my ships,— yea, e'en the clamorous light
That threats destruction from the heart of heaven,

Awaits my call.   More swift than Mercury,
He flashes up and round the whirling globe,
My fiery messenger.   I have good cause
To walk erect, and worship none but him
Who fashioned me, a semblance of himself,
Creation's miracle.   I rule the earth
By license of divine authority :
The king of nature, and the son of God.

Consolation.

If you are shiftless
And therefore thriftless,
You may nevertheless stand high
In your own esteem — and why?
You pause?
Because
A god holds you down and a god lifts your
        brother ;
Misfortune is one god and fortune the other.
You are as able as he and drown,
For you have no luck :
Your friend has no merit, but fortune makes him
Swim like a duck.

The Sparrows and the Lark.

Hundreds of quick little sparrows were scratch-
    ing a heap near the barn door,
Which the good farmer had thrown out of his
    horse's stall.
Quarrelsome fellows they were, and incessant
    their noise and their flutter;
Orators every one, — listeners, oh, no, not
    here.
Soon they discovered a skylark hid in the leaves
    of a myrtle;
Cocksparrow bold, with a chirp, hopped on the
    share of a plow.
Say, you proud songster, come down, and par-
    take of our jollification.
Why be so lonely and sad? Come, you shall sing
    us a song.
Ah, my good sparrow, believe me, I like not the
    smell of your dunghill;
For when I sing I must soar swiftly aloft toward
    the sun.
Here my poor vision is narrow, while high in the
    realm of the ether,
Mountain and forest and sea calmly repose in my
    eye. —
What is the good of your song, if no one can
    follow to hear it?

Surely a song never heard, is but a song never
     sung.—

Wisely you speak it, O sparrow, and that is the
     key to my sadness:

Happy indeed were the lark, if all the sparrows
     could fly.

Still, little practical friend, my song is not
     utterly wasted ;

The eagle, the clouds and the sun, dwell in the
     reach of my song.

The Two Pines.

Here in the forest, I look on the manifold tribe of
     the pine tree,

Family large as of man ; like and unlike too, as
     well.

Needles and twigs and a trunk, they possess both
     alone, and in common,

Merely, they differ in size — stay and consider
     again.

Here is a wee little fellow, a pigmy, forsooth, of
     the family,

One you might carry away, plant in a pot like a
     flower.

Dressed in the color of spring, in the merry
     green garment of nature,

Smiling he looks on himself, perfect, however so
     small.

Why should he dread the loud clamor of lightning and thunder in heaven?
Why should he fear the great wind sweeping a
tempest above?
Elements, battling on high, never tarry to smite
him with fire,
And the fierce rush of the wind strips not one
needle from him.
Strong in his weakness he stands, unknown and
unknowing he prospers,
Circles complete as the sun, there on an inch of
the soil. —
Yonder, you see, is his brother, a giant of
mighty dimensions;
Grand and majestic he rules, lifting his crown to
the sun.
Dreary and dry is his trunk, and there at his foot,
you may gather
Infinite needles and twigs, shaken adown by the
storm.
Many dead branches are reaching like withered
arms from his body:
Once they were lusty and green, now they must
perish, because
The hungry head doth absorb all the food that
the sunlight would give them;
Starved and neglected they droop, patiently wait-
ing to die.
See, where the woodman is come, the director
supreme of the forest;

Sharp is the edge of his ax, mighty the strength
  of his arm.
Thorough the flesh and the bone he smites the
  keen blade of his weapon:
Hark, how the echo resounds!   Sullen the giant
  endures.
Now he is struck to the heart; he shivers, he
  moans and he totters,
Tumbles, and crashing to earth, thunders aloud
  in his fall.
Such, O my friend, is his fate: not his life, but
  his death, will contribute
Rafter and beam to your house, timber and mast
  to your ship.

Brook and Ocean.

Why is the ocean so dark, and why is the brook
  so transparent?
Both are but water, I ween — solve me this rid-
  dle, I pray.
There in the crystalline current I see to its very
  foundation,
Castles and turrets I see, shimmering gay in the
  sun.
Valleys and hillocks of sand may be traced in
  this little creation;
Ranges of pebble and stone rise like the Alps to
  my view.

And forests I see in the brook, for the weeds and
    the flags and the rushes
Thrive like the mightiest wood. Fishes, I too
    can discern,
With golden and silvery scales, as they gambol
    and glint in the water,
Hiding and seeking — who knows? Haply no
    less than ourselves.
Truly, this magical runnel reveals a whole world
    to my vision :
Landscape and life I behold, clear and transparent
    and true.
But when I've gone to the ocean to peer in his
    infinite waters,
Nothing but darkness I saw. Tell me, oh, tell
    me, why is it?
Chide not the ocean, my friend, because thy
    ambition was baffled;
Blame but the ken of thine eye : thou art too
    feeble to see.
Dip with a cup from the ocean, and dip with a
    cup from the runnel,
Here is the great and the small: both will appear
    as of one.
Thus thou may'st compass the all, by seizing a
    part of it only :
Set thy dry lips to the brook, seek not to swallow
    the sea.

The Devil.

Tell me, oracular maiden, for why was the devil
    created?
God is good, and the world sprang from his
    goodness and grace.
God is almighty as well, and therefore the deeds
    of the devil
Stand as the deeds of the Lord, done by his
    creature, his will.
I have been told, he was sent to punish our sins,
    but look you,
He is the root of that sin, therefore the answer
    falls short.
I do not speak of the monster with horns and
    hoofs and a pitchfork,
But of our frailty, our faults; yea, of the devil
    in us.—
That is the devil, indeed, the spirit of death and
    denial,
Who with temptation or pain meets us wherever
    we go.
But if all ills were abolished, then could man no
    longer do evil;
Then, too, the good of his deed were not his
    freedom, but fate.
Now, being free he may choose, may become, as
    it were, his own maker:

Here is the evil and good, take whichsoever thou
wilt.

Life were insipid and dull unless the quick devil
defied us ;

Ever must he arise, ever must thou put him
down.—

Thank thy Creator, oh man, for thou truly art
blessed with the devil:

How couldst thou conquer the fiend, if he had
never been born?

Optimism.

I am a priest of the sun and no sorrow shall cloud
my good spirits,

Yet overnight I was cast deep in a visional gloom.

For in my dream I beheld the pale ghost of
eternal mutation,

Ruling within and without, ruling above and
below.

Still the rude spectre pursues me, for all I can see
and can think of

Shrinks into nothing and fades, touched by his
wand of decay.

Nothing endures, and our birth is simply the
cause of our burial ;

Every thing that exists tells us, it shall not exist.

Kingdoms and peoples have perished, the universe ever is changing,

Arts and philosophies, too, burnt like ephemeral
    sparks.

Religion itself is perverted in this everlasting
    mutation :

Are not the gods of the past, idols and falsehoods
    to us?

Weary and sick is my heart, for no matter what
    truth I may conquer,

Next day proves it a lie — was and has been —
    nothing now.

That is enough, foolish fellow, thy reason is
    sorely benighted,

Else thou the answer hadst read, writ in each
    word thou hast said :

If all things are subject to change, why then too
    the change must be changing ;

Change the change, and thou hast permanence.—
    Dost thou conceive?

Epigrams.

Cap not your proofs with a proverb; their wisdom is mighty deceptive,
And your rival may read backward as well and as
 true.

The means and the ends of thy life be both con-
 sistent with honor:
Honor the means as a part, honor the ends as
 the all.

Money is king of the world, and worldlings are
 bondmen to money;
Still, there is infinite wealth, free from his tyran-
 nous rule.

Nay, I condemn not your labor, but see that you
 work not for nothing;
Most of us might have achieved double the pay
 for our pains.

Mere acquisition appears to be the great goal of
 the many;
See, how it dwindles away when application
 appears.

Yes, I approve your ambition, but rate not this
    money too highly;
Pitiful poor is the man coining his life into gold.

Truly the kingdom of joy is not ruled by the
    monarchs of money;
Spirits of blessed content, need not a housing of
    gold.
Felicity yields to no bribe, but your money can
    furnish
Many a trifle and trick, many a pleasure and
    whim.

Shall I present you the man that is borne on the
    full tide of fortune?
He whose employment pursues, merely the bent
    of his mind.

Tender your ear to the wise, for their discord is
    all a delusion;
Learn but the soul of their song, concord divine
    you will hear.

Show me the purpose of man, and tell me his
    noblest ambition:
Liberty! — but have a care, liberty means not
    caprice.

Able and honest opinions will join the most dar-
  ing opponents;
Only the stupid and false wrangle and cannot
  agree.

Discord proclaims imperfection, for liberty and
  compulsion,
Selfish and generous deeds, are but a unit with
  God.

Pity not, envy the man, that is moved by a breath
  of displeasure:
Hearts that are racked with a storm, feel not the
  cursory breeze.

Weary me not with your sermons of good and of
  evil behavior:
Virtue and vice are but one, speaking in general
  terms.
Show me a case in particular, bring me all cause
  and condition,
Then I will try to decide, if it be good or
  be ill.

Law is no limit to greatness, but we must endure in its confines:
Crimes that Achilles confessed will not be par-
doned in you.
Cæsar once stole the whole earth, and his fame
shall continue forever;
Jack will be sent to the jail, if he but pilfer a
loaf.

Be not a cynic, my friend, nor condemn this
imperfect existence,
Tutor thy soul to imbibe draughts from the
infinite spring.
Many a charming nymph you will find on the
marge of the fountain,
Many a sage old man,— beauty and wisdom,
what more?

Young Alexander bemoaned the triteness of
earthy dimensions;
Aged Diogenes found pleasure to bask in the sun.

Strive to acquire an object for which thou
wouldst willingly perish;
Only from that moment on hast thou good reason to live.

If thou hast nothing more dear to thee than
    existence,
Then thou already art dead, buried ignobly in
    flesh.

Man and woman are two. Preserve their dis-
    tinction, I charge you :
Opposite poles give a spark — mere repetition
    repels.

Shakespeare was written by Bacon, old Goethe
    oft slipped in his morals,
Homer, perhaps, never lived. There, I am done
    with ye all !

Some of us love the great books, but most of us
    still avoid them.
Is it for fear we might learn what we already
    should know?

Homer I saw in a bookstore, the price not so
    much as your dinner :
Pennies will purchase a world, millions can yield
    you no more.

Miracles are of the past, and our mighty Creator
　　no longer
Stretches adown his right arm, giving us proof of
　　his power.
Look you, a wonder more strange than the sun
　　standing still on the hill-top,
Lies in the wisdom divine, forcing him ever to
　　move.

Somehow I can not persuade me, that Christ
　　could have walked on the water.
Well, then he did not for you; but for some
　　others he did.

Paradise was to the beast, for it fell when man's
　　wit was created.
That was a wonderful fall, fall from below to
　　above.

Somehow I trust not the man who banks on the
　　doctrine of mercy:
Faith in the mercy of God, renders him apter to
　　sin.

Christ did not teach a religion, a creed, nor a
　　church, nor a dogma.
Said not Saint Paul to the Greeks, " all too relig-
　　ious ye are? "

Mark, how in ages long past, man feared or was
strange to his deity.
Christ was the first to reveal participation in God.

Truth is the aim of the arts, of philosophy and of
religion :
All, though by different paths, strive to the same
great end.

TRANSLATIONS FROM GOETHE.

(89)

The Rosebud on the Heather.

Once a boy a rosebud spied,
　　Rosebud on the heather:
There it bloomed in virgin pride,
Quickly to the spot he hied,
　　Loved it altogether.
Rosebud, rosebud, rosebud red,
　　Rosebud on the heather.

Said the boy : " I'll pluck thee, too,
　　Rosebud on the heather ! "
Said the rose : " And, if you do,
I will sting, and thou shalt rue
　　This offense forever."
Rosebud, rosebud, rosebud red,
　　Rosebud on the heather.

And the boy in passion wrung
    Rosebud from the heather;
Rosebud struggled, wept and stung ;
All in vain, the wild boy wrung
    Thorns and rose together.
Rosebud, rosebud, rosebud red,
    Rosebud on the heather.

Found.

Alone I sauntered
    Through shadowy wood;
In search of nothing,
    In tranquil mood.

In vale sequestered
    I spied afar
A flower, glistening
    Like diamond star.

I stooped to pluck it,
    When soft it said:
Shall I to wither
    Be plucked, and dead?

With all its rootlets
    I dug it out,
That in my garden
    It still might sprout.

And there I set it
With tender care;
It thrives as ever,
And blooms as fair.

The Shepherd.

He was a lazy keeper,
A dreamy Seven-sleeper,
Cared little for his sheep.

A damsel need but touch him,
When misery would clutch him :
No appetite, no sleep.

He roamed with heart encumbered,
The midnight stars he numbered,
Did little else than weep.

Now, that the damsel took him,
He found all that forsook him :
Thirst, appetite and sleep.

To Luna.

Sister of the pristine light,
Image fair of love in mourning!
Silvery mists thy face adorning
Float about thy visage bright;

Thy soft footfall, fairy light,
Wakes from caves and dayless holes,
Wandering, woe-departed souls,
Me, and ghostly birds of night.

Searchingly thy glances glide
O'er a grandly measured distance.
Grant the dreamer thy assistance,
Lift me, goddess, to thy side!
And in amorous delight,
Would the tempest-driven lover
Peer through bars and lattice cover,
See his loved one, night for night.

Contemplation's ecstasy
Soothes the distant lover's sorrow;
And thy shining beams I borrow,
And with Argus' eyes I see.
Bright and brighter, more and more,
All her beauty lies unshielded,
Draws me down, as you once yielded
To Endymion's charms of yore.

A Lover's Longing.

I think of thee, when merry sunlight dances
    Upon the deep ;
I think of thee, when Luna's quivering glances
    In fountains sleep.

I see thee, love, when far the distant highway
    Is wrapt in dust ;
In dead of night, when through a lonely by-way,
    The wanderer must.

I hear thee, love, when surgy billows tumble
    With ceaseless moan ;
In shaded glen, where all is hushed and humble,
    I list alone.

I am with thee; and wert thou e'er so distant,
    Thou still art near !
The sun is set, the stars begin to glisten,
    Would thou wert here !

Calm at Sea.

Weary silence rules the water,
Not a ripple roughs the main;
And the sailor peers disheartened
O'er the endless, glassy plain.
Not a breath from any quarter!
Drowsy death lies on the deep!
In the wide and viewless water,
Wind and wave are fast asleep.

Admonition.

Wilt thou ever ramble further?
　See, the good lies all so near:
Do but learn to grapple fortune,
　Her delights are ever here.

May Song.

All nature sparkles
  In pristine light!
The sun refulgent!
  The fields how bright!

Quick blossoms labor
  In bush and tree,
And song-birds carol
  Their jubilee;

And joy and rapture
  Expand the breast.
O earth, O heaven,
  O sunlight blest!

O love, O longing!
  So golden bright;
Like break of morning
  On yonder height!

You shower a blessing
  On teeming lands;
With crescent fervor
  The world expands.

7

O maiden, maiden,
  My heart is thine!
Thine eyes give answer!
  Thy heart is mine!

So loves the lark
  High heaven's blue,
So blossoms love
  The glist'ning dew,

As I, with eager
  And warm delight,
Love thee, sweet maiden,
  Who day and night

Plays on my heartstrings
  In measured rhyme.
Be ever happy
  As thou art mine!

The Shepherd's Lament.

I stand on the hill-top yonder,
  A thousand times, I know,
Upon my crook-staff bending,
  And gaze on the valley below.

I follow the sheepflocks grazing,
  My shepherd dog watches them well;
I've dropped from the hill to the valley,
  But how, I can scarcely tell.

The meadow is brightly spangled
  With blossoms of brilliant hue;
I pick them, but all without knowing
  Whom I shall give them to.

In thunder, rain and in lightning,
  I stand by a sheltering tree.
The door of yon house will not open;
  'Tis only a phantom I see.

A rainbow is airily guarding
  The house, with its prismical band!
But she, who lived there, has wandered
  Far into a distant land;

Far over the land and further,
  Perhaps e'en over the seas.
Move onward, ye sheep, move onward,
  The shepherd is ill at ease.

To the Moon.

Now again o'er bush and dell
   Floats thy misty light,
And at last thy magic spell
   Frees my bosom's night.

Down the vista of my past
   Soothingly you look,
Like a friend, thine eye is cast
   On my fated book.

Echoes far from days of old
   Steal into mine ear,
Paradise and pain untold,
   Greet me, wandering here.

River dear, flow on, flow on;
   Like thy spumy froth,
Jest and kiss, for aye, have gone,
   And her plighted troth.

Still, there was a time, when I
   Love's delights possessed;
And remembrance with a sigh
   Still disturbs my rest.

Rush, dear river, rush along,
   Neither stop nor stay,
Rush and whisper to my song
   Thy melodious lay,

When thy billows surge and rave
  In the wintry night,
Or thy tepid waters lave
  Vernal blossoms bright.

Blesséd he, who without hate,
  Shuns the world's great noise,
To his bosom clasps a friend,
  And with him enjoys

What, unknown to mortal man,
  Journeys by thy light,
Through the bosom's labyrinth
  In the stilly night.

Sledge or Anvil.

Mark my words, and do not grumble:
Struggle in life's early hour
To be wise and to be free;
In the'scales of fortune's power,
Fixéd balance can not be :
You must climb or you must tumble,
You must conquer and then king it,
Or must slave and lose it all ;
Swim or sink, or rise or fall,
Sledge or anvil you must be.

Vanitas! Vanitatum Vanitas!

My heart is set on nothing now,
    Hurra!
The world may wag, I care not how,
    Hurra!
Whoever would my companion be,
Lift high his bumper and sing with me.
Set the last bottle free!

My heart was set on goods and gold,
    Hurra!
And then my summer mood caught cold,
    Oh psha!
The coin kept rolling far and near,
And when I tried to seize it here,
There it would disappear.

On women next I set my heart,
    Hurra!
And hell on earth was all my part,
    Oh psha!
The false one led me by the nose,
The true one palled, as dull as prose,
The best, another chose.

I set my heart on travel then,
    Hurra!
And left my home, my countrymen,
    Oh psha!

And I was always ill at ease,
The beds were bad, and big the fees,
And the food worse than these.

I set my heart on honor's store,
  Hurra!
And see, another soon had more,
  Oh psha!
When I attained to high degree,
The people began to squint at me,
Tried but my faults to see.

I set my heart on thundering war,
  Hurra!
With gun and sword we traveled far,
  Hurra!
We conquered the foe, and forged his chains,
But friends were lost, and for my pains
Only one leg remains.

And now on nothing my heart is set,
  Hurra!
And mine's the world from rise to set,
  Hurra!
Now song and feast have come to end;
But e'en the dregs let us befriend,
Till the last drop descend.

The Angler.

The waters flow'd, the waters swell'd,
　Upon the brink he lay,
And calmly viewed the line he held
　And watch'd the wavelets play.
And as he lies and listens there,
　The restless floods unclose:
And from the waves, bewitching fair,
　A dripping sea-nymph rose.

She sang to him, she spoke to him,
　" Why dost thou lure my brood,
With human wit and human guile,
　Out of their native flood?
Ah, if thou knew'st how merrily
　We frolic there below,
You'd come to us, and verily,
　I'd heal thy bossom's woe.

The sun and sister moon delight
　To see their mirrored face:
He comes by day, and she by night
　To Neptune's cool embrace.
Art thou not moved by this deep sky,
　So fathomless, so blue?
Not by thy image floating by,
　Wash'd in eternal dew? ''

The waters flow'd, the waters swell'd,
  They laved his naked feet;
Soft longings in his bosom well'd,
  He saw his true-love greet.
She spoke to him, she sang to him,
  Resistless was her strain,
Half drew she him, half sank he in,
  And ne'er was seen again.

The King in Thule.

There was a king in Thule,
  All faithful to the grave,
To whom his dying mistress
  A golden goblet gave.

He prized no jewel better
  Than this beloved cup;
A glistening tear would gather
  Whene'er he took it up.

And as his days were ending
  He gave all to his heir,
His sceptre and his cities,
  But not the goblet, rare.

High in his sea-washed castle,
In proud ancestral hall,
He sat at kingly table,
Surrounded by his thrall.

*

There stood the old carouser,
Drank Bacchus' golden blood,
And cast the sacred beaker
Down to the seething flood.

He saw it dropping, drinking,
And sinking in the main.
His eyelids closed forever,
Drank never a drop again.

The Youth and the Mill-race,

YOUTH.

Where are you going, little brook,
So sprightly?
You run with clear and laughing look,
So lightly.
What is't you seek in yonder lea?
I prithee stop and speak to me.

MILL-RACE.

I was a brooklet once, good sir,
But look ye,
Into a ditch so narrow here
They took me,
That full and swift I run, until
They make me work in yonder mill.

YOUTH.

You skip along contentedly
To labor,
Know'st not the pain that troubles me,
Thy neighbor.
I ween, the miller's pretty lass
Looks often in thy watery glass.

MILL-RACE.

At blush of dawn she daily seeks
Her duty,
And comes to bathe her dimpled cheeks'
Soft beauty.
Her bosom swells so full and white,
I steam and bubble at the sight.

YOUTH.

If to the water she imparts
Desire,
How shall I quench my human heart's
Hot fire?
A single look, and then 'tis done,
One's peace of mind is ever gone.

MILL-RACE.

Then plunging on the wheel I dash
My powers,
And all the paddles whirl and splash
In showers.
Since e'er the maid is busy here,
The water works with better cheer.

YOUTH.

Ah brook, caus't thou not feel the stress
As we do?
She laughs at thee and cries in jest,
God speed you!
And yet, methinks, her amorous look
Might even check thy haste, O brook.

MILL-RACE.

I am so loth, so loth to go
From hither,
I wind my way now there, and flow
Now thither.
And if I had my choice, good sir,
I quickly would run back to her.

YOUTH.

Farewell, companion of a pain
I treasure;
Some day, perchance, you'll sing a strain
Of pleasure.
Go, straightway to my love impart,
What secret longing moves my heart.

Mismatched.

Even a couple divine discovered itself mismated:
Psyche grew older and wise, Cupid is ever a
child.

Apology.

Say not that woman is fickle in wavering from
one to another!
All this endeavor she spends, seeking a constant
man.

Elegy III.

Let not thy pride, sweet girl, feel ashamed at thy
    speedy surrender!
Trust me, I think thee not bold, think none the
    less of thee for it.
Cupid hath many a dart and different: some
    scratch but a little,
And their poisonous sting rankles for years in
    the heart;
Others are mightily feather'd, and tipped with his
    heavenly fire,
Burn their path to the bone, kindling with rap-
    ture the blood.
In the heroic great age, when goddess and god
    were enamored,
Then to behold was to crave, then was to crave
    to enjoy.
Think'st thou, the goddess of love delayed for a
    while to consider,
When she in Ida's cool shade saw that Anchises
    was fair?
Truly, had Luna neglected to kiss the adorable
    sleeper,
Envious Aurora's caress quickly had wakened
    the youth.
Hero's bright eyes met Leander's, and now the
    passionate lover
Plunges with setting sun, down to the Hellespont's
    flood.

Rhea Sylvia sauntered, the princely virgin, to
    draw
Tiber's water, and there she was embraced by the
    god.
Thus did Olympian Mars beget himself sons! —
    A wolfbitch
Suckles the twins, and Rome calls herself queen
    of the world.

Elegy X.

Alexander and Cæsar and Henry and Frederick,
    the mighty,
Gladly on me would bestow half their immortal
    renown,
Could I, to each of them, grant this couch for a
    single night's pleasure;
But the poor wretches are held deep in the realm
    of the shades.
Therefore, O mortal, rejoice in the blessing of
    love's warm passion;
Soon will thy fugitive foot shiver in Lethe's
    wave.

A Lover's Letter.

Wherefore I take my pen to hand again?
Thou must not, dearest, ask that so directly :
My letter brings no news, but serves correctly,
For it will reach my loved one's touch and ken.

Because I can not come, let this my sending,
Convey my love to thee in bootless fashion,
My bliss, hopes, ecstasies, joys, torments, pas-
  sion —
But this has no beginning and no ending.

I'll not confide to thee of this day's doing,
How in reflection, fancies and desire
My faithful heart essays to be with thee :

Thus I stood by thee once, thy face reviewing,
And spoke no word.   What words did I require?
My soul's contentment could no greater be.

The Goblet.

With embracing hands I held a goblet,
Deftly carved and filled by golden Bacchus ;
From its rim, I drained the beaded potion
In one draught, to drown all grief and sorrow.

Cupid softly entered, and surveyed me
With a modest smile upon his visage,
As in pity of the foolish fellow.

" Friend, I know a far more fairer vessel,
Worthy to absorb thy inmost spirit ;
What requital, if I bring it to thee,
Fill it for thee with a different nectar?"

Oh, how kindly Cupid kept his promise,
When you, Lida, moved by his persuasion,
Gently yielded to your pining lover.

When with rapture I embrace thy body,
And from lips unkissed by any other,
Drink the balm of thy long-stored affection,
Then in bliss I commune with my spirit:

Such a vessel never yet was fashioned,
Nor possessed by any god save Cupid.
Vulcan never from his shining marble
Carved.such harmony with gifted chisel.
On his vine-clad mountains, may Lyaeus,
With his fauns, the wisest and most ancient,
Press the clusters of his grapes celestial,
Guide himself the mystic fermentation;
Wine like this, no skill of his can furnish.

Cupid as a Landscape Painter.

Sat I on a rocky peak one morning,
Gazed with fixed eyes into the vapor;
Like a canvas with a grayish background,
It arose before me and above me.

Suddenly a boy appeared beside me,
Saying: " Gentle friend, why art thou gazing
With indifference on the empty canvas?
Can it be, that thou hast lost thy passion
To create in plastic and in picture? "

Looking on the child, I thought in secret:
" Hem, the lad presumes to play the master."

" While you thus continue sad and idle,"
Said the youngster, " it will come to nothing:
Come, I'll paint a little picture for thee,
Teach thee, how to paint a pretty picture."

And he pointed with his index finger,
Like a blushing rose was its complexion,
To the wide interminable canvas,
Started then to sketch with rosy finger:

First on high a radiant sun he painted,
Shining mightily into my vision,
And the clouds he touched with golden lining,
Made the glinting sunbeams dance between them.

Painted then the tree-tops, delicately,
Of a dew-gemmed forest, traced the hill-tops
Just behind them, one beside the other;
Underneath he left no lack of water,
Sketched the river so precise to nature,
That it seemed to glitter in the sunlight,
That it seemed to rush along its margin.

Ay, and flowers bloomed beside the river,
And the meadow teemed in living colors,
Gold and green and red and blue and purple,
Sparkling all, like emeralds and rubies.

Then the lambent sky he deftly shaded,
And the azure mountains far and further,
So that I enrapt and re-created,
Looked upon the painter and the picture.

"Now, at least," he said, "I have convinced
    thee,
That I am no tyro in this business ;
But the hardest still remains before me."

Thereupon he sketched with pointed finger
Heedfully, beside the little forest,
Just upon its boundary, where the sunlight
Shone reflected on the luscious greensward,
Sketched a most bewitching, lovely maiden,
Well proportioned, gracefully attired,
Dimpled cheeks beneath her auburn tresses,
And the cheeks were of the self-same color
As the dainty finger, that produced them.

"Tell me, boy," I cried, " who was thy master,
That so speedily and true to nature,
Thou could'st first arrange it all so wisely,
Then complete it all to such perfection?"

As I spoke these words, a gentle zephyr
Fluttered lightly in the leafy tree-tops,
Rippled all the waves upon the river,
Filled the veil of my consummate maiden,
And what made me, wondering, still more wonder,
Was to see the maid herself in motion,

See her to the very spot approaching,
Where I sat beside my wanton tutor.

Now, that all about me was in motion,
River, trees and flowers and the garment,
And the dainty feet of fairest maiden,
Do ye think, that on my rock I lingered
Like a rock, unmoved by all this motion?

The Frogs.

A pond was covered with ice and snow;
The little frogs, penned in the water below,
No longer were able to croak and spring;
But vowed to each other while half asleep,
Could they but rise from prison deep,
Like nightingales they would sweetly sing.—
A sunbeam came, unlocked the door,
They paddled and proudly hopped ashore,
And sat on the margin far and wide,
And croaked as ever, so woe-betide.

Different.

One day we sauntered side by side,
  Deep in the forest green;
I tried to kiss her, " Stop ! " she cried,
  " If you do that, I'll scream."

In rage I shouted: " Zounds ! I'll kill
  The man dares interfere ! "
" Hush ! dear," she whispered low, " be still !
  There may be some one near."

Ingenious Impulse.

I roll, howe'er the world may run,
  Like Saint Diogenes my tun.
Now I am serious, now in fun,
  Now love and seek, now hate and shun,
Now this, now that, is tried, begun,
  Sometimes 'tis something, sometimes none.
I roll, howe'er the world may run,
  Like Saint Diogenes my tun.

To an Original.

A quidam says: " I recognize no system!
No master lives to whom I listen;
And I am proud as proud can be,
That dead men never tutored me."
That means, if I am not mistaken,
" I am an ass of my own making."

The Way of the World.

When I was a youngster, devil-may-care,
Happy and go as you please,
No painter or sculptor did ever declare,
That my features were likely to please.
But many a bonny lass I knew,
Whose lips were sweet, whose heart was true.
Now as I sit here, a master and old,
My name is sounded in every land;
On pipes and platters I am sold,
Like ancient Fritz on every hand.
But the maidens fair remain afar;
O dream of youth!   O golden star!

Sayings in Rhyme.

If to infinity you would stride,
Walk in the finite on every side.

The universe may be your feast,
If you can discover the all, in the least.

Why boys with girls delight to dance?
Extremes will meet at every chance.

That man in safe condition rests,
Who carries out his own behests.

If you stretch longer than your sheet,
You'll find yourself with naked feet.

Kissed lips and the new moon
Convalesce soon.

How excellently all would chime,
If we could do 't a second time.

———

They simply say: I like it not!
And then they think it's gone to pot.

———

We treat a matter in conversation,
With ample reflection and long hesitation,
And in the end, an evil " must "
Concludes the question in disgust.

———

However your deed, successful and good,
May be met by an enemy's carping mood,
Sooner or later, to his shame,
He'll will he, nill he, do the same.

———

If you have been wronged by a noble man,
Dismiss it from memory, as quick as you can:
He'll think of it to the very letter,
And will not long remain your debtor.

———

Ivy and a tender heart
Lovingly cling with gentle art.
If they can find neither trunk nor wall,
They must wither and wilt and fall.

Whom shall we call Dame Fortune's favorite
    son?
Who gladly labors, and enjoys what's done.

I know of no greater advantage on earth,
Than to perceive my enemy's worth.

A masquerade is not the place
To take the visor from your face.

Fortune's whole troop
Cannot help the loon :
If rain were soup,
He'd have no spoon.

This mundane sphere is not a gruel-stew ;
A lotus-eater's life one cannot follow :
There be many tough bits to chew,
And we must choke or swallow.

Tame Xenia.

Leave we the temporal,
Whate'er it be !,
Ourselves to immortalize
Is the decree.

" Why do you slightly heed
All that is done? "
We live in the deed,
What's done, is done.

" You speak of immortality :
Let's have your reasons, for we doubt it."
One reason is, mortality
Can never get along without it.

" Who is a useless man, I pray? "
One that knows neither how to command nor
    obey.

Jackdaws screech about the people
That are the buttons on the steeple.

How busily they pry and pother,
With thinking they are all undone.
They'd like to find an answer, other
Than his, who has the proper one.

———————

What women love, what women hate,
Shall be their privilege sans debate ;
But when they try to judge and reason,
Methinks, they're clearly out of season.

———————

The student of science and art
Has likewise religion ;
Whoever has neither science nor art,
Should have religion.

———————

" Why as with a broom, pray tell me,
Were these kings swept out of door? "
Had they been real kings, I tell ye,
They might still have held the floor.

Sayings in Prose.

All things wise have already been thought, one must merely endeavor to think them again.

———

In the works of man, as in those of nature, it is really the intentions, that deserve foremost consideration.

———

If I am to listen to the opinion of another, it must be expressed positively; of the problematical I have enough in myself.

———

Certain books seem to have been written, not for the purpose of teaching anything, but rather to inform us, that the author knew something.

———

Many a man taps about the wall with a hammer, and imagines that he hits the nail on the head every time.

———

Writing history, is a way to rid one's self of the past.

What we do not understand, we do not possess.

Instead of contradicting my words, they should act according to my purport.

Snow is a sham cleanliness.

It is said: vain self-praise smells: that may be; but for the odor of alien and unjust censure, the public has no nose.

The puddle glistens when the sun shines.

The miller imagines, that wheat grows merely to supply his mill.

The Hindoos of the desert vow to eat no fish.

Wise men have much in common.—Aeschylus.

It is the most foolish of all errors, when clever young heads fear to lose their originality, by acknowledging a truth, which others have acknowledged before them.

It is much easier to detect an error, than to find the truth: the former lies at the surface, and there is little difficulty with that; the latter dwells in the depth; to search for it, is not every one's affair.

If one demands duties without conceding rights, one must pay well.

Ingratitude is always a kind of weakness. I have never noticed that able men have been ungrateful.

A prudent man is not subject to slight follies.

Error evermore repeats itself in action: therefore one must untiringly repeat the truth in words.

" The Greeks, of all peoples, have dreamed the dream of life most beautifully."

That is true symbolism, where the particular represents the universal, not as a dream and shadow, but as the living instantaneous revelation of the inscrutable.

On acquiring freedom all men assert their defects ; the strong exaggerate, the week neglect.

What government is the best? That which teaches us to govern ourselves.

There is nothing more terrible than an active ignorance.

It makes quite a difference, whether a poet seeks the particular for the universal, or beholds the universal in the particular. The former results in allegory, wherein the particular passes as a mere instance or example of the universal; the latter, on the other hand, is really the nature of poesy, uttering the particular, without thought or reference to the universal. Now, whosoever seizes this particular in its life, receives at the same time the universal, without becoming aware of it, or at least not until late.

The world takes every man as he shows himself; but he must show himself as something. We had rather endure an inconvenient person, than tolerate an insignificant one.

We do not become acquainted with people when they come to us; we must go to them, to learn how matters stand with them.

Voluntary dependency is the most beautiful of all conditions, and how were that possible without love!

Against the great advantages of another, the only remedy is love.

No man is more enslaved, than he who mistakingly considers himself free.

One cannot more surely evade the world than through the arts, and one can not more surely link himself to her, than through the arts.

To express one's self is nature; to receive expressions as they are given, is culture.

Nothing more marks a man's character, than that which he finds absurd.

The understanding finds almost everything absurd; reason, almost nothing.

There are but two true religions; one, which entirely without form, the other, which in the fairest form, acknowledges and worships what is holy within and about us. All that lies between is idolatry.

We are never deceived, we deceive ourselves.

All laws were framed by the aged and by men. Youths and women desire the exception, old men the rule.

It is not sufficient to know, we must also apply; it is not sufficient to wish, we must also act.

Did we put ourselves in the place of others, the hatred and jealousy we so often harbor against them, would fall away; and did we put others in our place, pride and conceit would decrease considerably.

Modern poets mix a great deal of water with their ink.

———

Does the sparrow then know the stork's frame of mind?

———

Whoever misses the first button-hole, will not come out right with his buttoning.

———

Our adversaries think they disprove our arguments, when they reiterate their own opinion, without paying the least attention to ours.

———

The problem which aspiring men find hard to solve is, to acknowledge the merits of older contemporaries, and not permit themselves to be handicapped by their shortcomings.

———

There is a germ of temerity in every artist, without which talent is inconceivable. This germ quickens especially when we circumscribe and cramp a capable man, wishing to hire and use him for one-sided purposes.

Whoever intends to accuse an author of obscurity, should first scrutinize his own inner self, to see whether it be well illuminated there. In the dusk, very clear print becomes illegible.

Peculiarity in expression, is the beginning and the end of all art.

Ignorant people raise questions, which wise men have answered a thousand years ago.

Man must abide in the belief, that the incomprehensible may be comprehended: otherwise he would cease to investigate.

Whatsoever one knows, one really knows only for himself. If I speak to another of that which I believe I know, he immediately believes to know it better, and I am compelled to retire with my knowledge into my inner self.

The age has advanced: every individual, however, starts from the beginning.

Indulge the woman in her will!
  From a crooked rib was she create,
God could not make her perfectly straight.
  Try to bend her, she will break;
Leave her, and she'll crook still worse;
  Which, Adam, is the greater curse?
Indulge the woman in her will;
  A broken rib will make you ill.

If the landscape I'm to show,
To the housetop you must go.

To the Countess Titinne O'Donnell, who requested one of
my writing quills.

When the schoolboy dutifully
With his satchel trudged to school,
And began to scribble, duly,
Letters with his feathered tool,
Then the goal of his ambition
Was to write a seemly hand:
That his writing had a mission,
Should receive wide recognition,
Yea, that e'en a price should rule
On his quills, the boy at school,
Sitting on his lowly stool,
Surely did not understand.

www.ingramcontent.com/pod-product-compliance
Lightning Source LLC
Chambersburg PA
CBHW060245030726
47493CB00025B/2318